The Care and Feeding of Fish

A story with pictures by Sarajo Frieden

Houghton Mifflin Company Boston 1996

All rights reserved. For information about permission to reproduce selections from this book, write to Permissions, Houghton Mifflin Company, 215 Park Avenue South, New York, New York 10003.

For information about this and other Houghton Mifflin trade and reference books and multimedia products, visit The Bookstore at Houghton Mifflin on the World Wide Web at http://www.hmco.com/trade/.

Manufactured in the United States of America • Book design by Sarajo Frieden and David Saylor • The text of this book is set in 14-point Monotype Amasis Medium • The illustrations are gouache, reproduced in full color.

WOZ 10 9 8 7 6 5 4 3 2 1

Library of Congress Cataloging-in-Publication Data   Frieden, Sarajo
The care and feeding of fish / by Sarajo Frieden.   p.   cm.
Summary: Following the instructions in an old notebook her great-aunt accidentally mailed to her, Loulou takes her pet fish to a tailor, to dancing school, and to tea, causing him to become the toast of the town.   ISBN 0-395-71251-3
[1. Fishes—Fiction.   2. Humorous stories.]   I. Title. PZ7.F8962Car   1996
[E]—dc20   94-38738   CIP   AC

For William
and Miro
Special thanks to
Sally
Lianne
Norma Jean
Judy
David

Loulou had always lived in the same house on the same street, stepping over the same sidewalk cracks every day on her way to school. She moved only once, a few doors away, but her mother and father took the house with them, so attached were they to the sameness of their lives. Nothing much ever happened, and Loulou's parents liked it that way.

But Loulou did not.
She longed for a life
of high adventure,
gallivanting around
the globe like her
great-aunt Eclair.

On the morning of Loulou's seventh birthday,
a large and well-traveled box arrived on her
doorstep. It was from her great-aunt, who was
on a fact-finding, fish-gathering expedition on
the tiny island of Tumba-Bumba.

Delighted that her great-aunt had not forgotten her birthday, Loulou opened the package and found a large and unusual fish inside. She immediately set about making her fish feel at home. In her haste, she failed to notice a mysterious leather notebook that had somehow found its way to the bottom of the box.

The next morning, Loulou woke to find that the fish had grown considerably overnight. In his lap lay the mysterious notebook:

THE CARE
AND FEEDING
OF FISH
TOP SECRET!
—— *by* ——
Professor Eclair de la Lune

Loulou was filled with curiosity about the notebook, but she tried not to give it another thought. Soon, of course, she could think of nothing else.

"A quick peek couldn't hurt," she said at last.
Bathed in the glow of her new fishbowl, she read:

Step One. Starting Out.
The first thing you must
do in the care and
feeding of your
fish is build a box.
Build it tall and
narrow or short
and fat
Put soft things
inside for padding and
don't forget to fasten
a lock on the outside.

Now gather all your previous notions about taking care of a fish and put them inside the box where they will be comfortable and you can forget about them. Lock the box and hide the key.

Loulou peered at the fish, trying to think of a suitable name. It wasn't easy. After all, they had just met.

No doubt you have chosen the perfect name for your fish. Write the name here:

Harold

"And I'm Loulou," said Loulou. "But my friends all call me Lou."

Step Three. Now that your fish has a name, it's time to introduce him to the world. A stroll in the park is a good way to begin.

It was a brilliant spring day and the park was swarming with people. At first Harold was very shy, but with Lou's help he began to feel right at home.

If it's a hot day, there's nothing more pleasant than a dip in a cool pool. As you know, fish are excellent swimmers. Just be sure he doesn't get carried away.

But if you want to get carried away, take him along to dance class.

Step Four. You are beginning to see how much fun it is to care for a fish in the proper way. Next, a little shopping is in order. With fish in tow, pay a visit to your tailor. The fish will need some formal clothes. And of course you will want to pick out something for yourself to wear. You never want to be upstaged by a fish.

Before long, Lou and Harold were going everywhere. Harold enjoyed everything—except fishing, which he refused to do.

Step Five. It is a well-known fact that fish travel in schools. Do not confuse this with a proper education— and remember to pack your fish a lunch.

Harold was a sensation at school! He was good at finger-painting and knew more about halibut than anyone else in class, but his musical talents were out of this world. He mastered the oboe and the timpani, and his kazoo playing was without peer. "He's quite a catch!" exclaimed Mrs. Metronome. Lou blushed with pride.

Overnight, Harold's popularity skyrocketed. Everyone in school wanted to invite him home for lunch. He was out all day and up all night, practicing his scales in the shower. And he never slept—fish, after all, don't have eyelids. Worst of all, he no longer had time for Lou. But she wasn't too worried. The notebook can help, she thought.

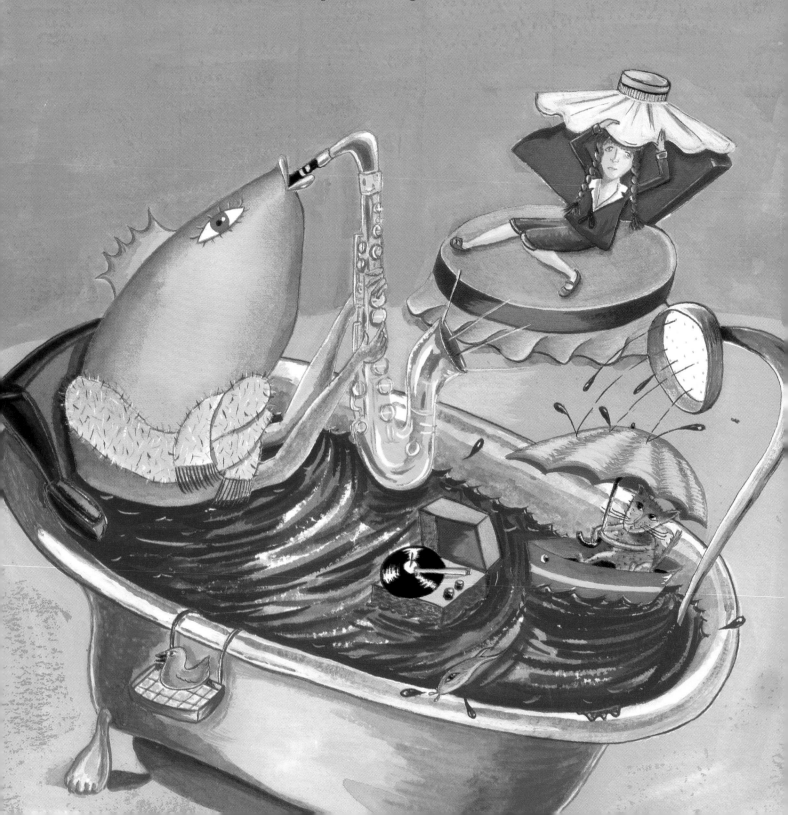

Step Six. Fish, having an extraordinary sense of hearing, are known for their love of opera. Do remember to bring plenty of hankies. Fish are very sensitive, and opera can be very sad.

Happy to be together again, Lou glanced at Harold during the performance, expecting to see him bored to the gills. He had a faraway look in his eyes and didn't notice her at all. Something had changed—Lou just didn't know what.

The next morning, Harold was nowhere to be found.
At first, Lou waited, hoping he would come home.
When she could stand it no longer, she turned to
the notebook.

*Lost and Found. In life, as in fishing,
the unpredictable can always happen.
If your hapless halibut has given you the
slip, don't hesitate. Call a professional.*

Lou went to the Bureau of Missing Persons, which sent her to the Office of Fishing Missions, which directed her to the Bureau of Fishy Persons, which, at last, sent her to the Inspector of Missing Fish.

Inspector Nemo sat in stunned silence while Lou told him the story of her life with Harold. "Young lady," the inspector said, "if half of what you're telling me is true, take my advice. Get another fish, then do something boring for a couple of years. . . . Next!"

When Lou returned home, she took out the box where she had stored her old notions and locked the notebook inside. "There will never be another Harold," she said sadly.

The next day, a package from Harold arrived with a note:

My dearest Loulou,

Tonight I sail for Italy on the S. S. Humongous *to pursue my dream of becoming a great opera singer. Please come to a farewell party. Thank you for helping me find my true calling. Love, Harold*

P.S. I hope you enjoy your new friend.

Later that day, Lou boarded
the ship. She heard the slow
strains of a violin and a
deep familiar voice, singing.
It was Harold, and he had
never looked happier.
Lou understood that
Harold was not
coming home.

That night, with Harold gone, the house seemed too quiet. From her bed, Lou watched her new fish swim peacefully around the fishbowl. It's almost like the old days, she thought as she drifted off to sleep, but something is missing. . . .